Inspired By

A NOVEL

Eddie Roy

ISBN 978-1-966540-23-6 (softcover)
ISBN 978-1-966540-21-2 (ebook)

This book is a work of fiction. Names, characters, places, and incidents are the product of the author's imagination or are used fictitiously. Any resemblance to actual locales, events, or persons, living or dead, is purely coincidental.

Printed in the United States of America.

INK START MEDIA
265 Eastchester Dr Ste 133 #102
High Point NC 27262

Inspired By

A NOVEL

Eddie Roy

CHAPTER 1

One More Red Carpet

On a clear, but breezy Hollywood Saturday night searchlights pierced the darkness, like huge swords of light being wielded by warriors dueling atop the theater's high-up roof. Guided by worn-out policemen, the nonstop stream of limos and town-cars that had rolled by for nearly an hour were now stopped while still fifty yards from where the cinema's entrance sat, or if already closer, at the policemen' instructions, they accelerated by, making way for the gaudy, dazzlingly bright silver-colored stretched Humvee limo that was slowly creeping up the congested street toward the massive, classically beautiful cinema that dominated nearly the entire block of the boulevard. Its traditional grandeur was unmissable even in the midst of the dozen other equally grand specimens of roaring-twenties excess that surrounded it. It featured something the neighboring buildings lacked: a huge marquee that spanned the full width of the structure, and was twenty feet up and extended from the building's front to the edge of the street. When the theater was first christened on its opening night in 1928; less than a full year before the stock market crashed, the newspaper's front-page headline had described the marquee as confidently challenging a single drop of rain to dampen the head of one of the theater's patrons.

None of the theater-goers that night dreamed that within a year a great many people would be lined up, not at theaters, but at soup kitchens. On that opening night, way back then, the marquee had displayed THE CIRCUS in bright lights. And beneath that: Charlie Chaplin. As it turned out, the weather had mattered not at all that night: opening night prove to be perfectly clear and comfortably cool, with not a drop of rain, nor even a cloud to hide the starlit sky. The theater's manager had proclaimed while cutting the ceremonial red ribbon while repeatedly forced to squint in the pulsing of flash-bulbs that, "The stars up there will never outshine the stars who will grace our movie screen for many years to come." In those days many of the largest theaters were built and owned by the movie studios. This particular moving-picture palace was created by Metro- Goldwin-Mayer more than fifty years before the man sipping champagne in the back of the silver limo was born.

Grant Sterling, all three hundred flabby pounds of him, sat slouched on the calf-leather seat in the back of the limo. After his second record breaking box-office blockbuster, one critic had taken a cheap shot at him, saying: "It's no wonder he produces hit movies: he has ample time to do it. He obviously spends his time on the couch and not the treadmill." Sterling had responded in an interview, "When they can't find anything wrong with my films, they get personal."

The fact that he carried the three hundred more like a sumo wrestler than like an NFL linebacker, bothered him not at all. He ate good because he could afford the best, and he deserved it. As the big vehicle neared the theater a roar of applause and cheers erupted as soon as the crowd caught sight of it. Everybody knew who was inside: Grant Sterling was very fond of "walking the dog" as his mother had called it. He simply considered it receiving his due recognition and admiration. His window was down so he could enjoy the applause that he was sure would greet him. He wasn't disappointed.

There was good reason for everybody to know whose limo it was. His publicist had made certain it was common knowledge when he'd purchased the limo the year before, as well as the fact that the car had been custom-painted a gleaming sterling-silver hue as his way of honoring himself. The luxurious black leather interior had silver accent panels. Evey one of the hundreds of lights shining that night reflected dazzling pinpoints of nearly blinding intensity from the car's surface.

As the big vehicle slowed to a halt with the door Grant Sterling would exit lined up precisely at the waiting red carpet, Sterling looked up at the marquee. That marvel of theatrical grandeur had fallen off the building during a massive storm back during the second world war. It was replaced by an even more dazzling one after the war, when people could again think about something other than world conflicts, and were again interested in, and could afford, to go to movies. It had been rebuilt and improved a dozen times in the years since. On this specific evening the words up in lights said:

LAST FLIGHT:
INSPIRED BY Actual EVENTS
WHAT HAPPENED TO FLIGHT 204?
And below that:

Grant Sterling was hoping to hit the trifecta with **Last Flight**. A third big hit would not only pay off the huge debt he'd piled up financing the film, but it would prove to the world that he was no flash-in the-pan. He hoped to prove the reality of the rule-of-thrice: "Once is a fluke, twice is a coincidence, thrice is a pattern." A third consecutive hit would confirm a pattern of him being a hit-maker.

His previous two movies: both monster hits, were so popular and such huge money-makers that this theater's management had invested the cash to have the decades-old marquee modified to include Sterling's back-lit logo to be displayed on the nights of his premiers. As a result, his movie premiers would not be held elsewhere. This theater was his domain. When his chauffer jumped from the driver's seat and dutifully opened his boss's door, Grant Sterling rolled out of the vehicle more than climbed out, while the driver stood close by to attempt to steady him should he lose his balance. A moment later a six-foot tall blond with plenty of store-bought curves and a five-thousand-dollar smile stepped lightly from the car door and stood behind him. She gave the moment a surreal look with the feel of a gazelle trailing behind a hippo.

A handful of years before, Grant Sterling had been just one of a hundred independent film-makers trying to be a break-out star in a nearly impossible field to become well-known in.

This film would make-or-break his image.

By the time he produced this movie: his third "Inspired by true events" film he'd gotten three times as adept at building nothing into something.

The real flight 204 was a plane transporting human organs for transplant. In the real world the plane had engine-trouble and slid off the end of the short runway at the only airport it could reach. The pilot suffered a mild concussion. No one else was injured and the organs weren't damaged.

When Grant Sterling's film hit the screen: terrorists had hijacked the plane, threatened to crash it into a hospital if not given a clear flight-path to Cuba. In Sterling's movie, the plane was shot down over the ocean by an Air Force fighter jet and the plane's pilot died when his parachute failed and he drowned. And at the end of the film Sterling himself delivered a heartfelt dedication to the seven people who died because they didn't receive the organs that went down with the plane.

The only thing true in the film was that there was a flight 204.

Grant Sterling considered the movie his crowning achievement. The premier would be the public's chance to judge what sort of legacy he was building.

CHAPTER 2
Sterling's History

A lucky day for Gant Sterling / a horrible day for nurses.

After he made four very average drama movies that barely broke even: and two of which went straight to home video, Grant Sterling was on the brink of bankruptcy. Then he picked up a newspaper one morning and read a front-page story about a multiple murder. Four college-age nurses, all employed by the same hospital, were driving to a party after finishing their evening shift. Before they reached the party site, a man had flagged them down by faking car trouble. Three of the four nurses didn't live long enough to scream. He cut their throats from ear-to-ear with a straight razor. The fourth nurse, the only survivor, stuck one of her inch-long fingernails in the man's left eye as soon as he got close enough to grab at her. According to the police report she said that she heard his eyeball pop like a cork being pulled from a bottle. The man shrieked and started running. Half-blind and in immense pain, he'd tripped over his own feet and gone face-down and screaming on the gravel shoulder of the road. Through streaming tears, the surviving nurse had meekly admitted to the police officer who interviewed her on-site that once the killer was on the ground screaming, she had kicked him in the head with all she had. The officer taking her report said, "Really, only once?"

She nodded and asked, "Am I in trouble for doing that?"

"Why would you think you'd be in trouble? The man just murdered three of your friends. It was self-defense"

"I practically blinded him, then kicked him in the head when he was down. Did I do anything wrong?"

The officer shook his head and answered, "Miss, I can't say this officially, but if I were you, I'd have kept kicking till he stopped screaming permanently."

The nurse answered, "I could have happily killed him, but it would have taken a lot of work and time. The officer had asked, "How's that?"

"Nurse's shoes are made with a soft sole, for silence, and also for all-day comfort. Not the perfect choice for caving in a man's skull. Then she'd shrugged before saying through tears, "I came real damn close to putting a finger-nail deep in his other eye, to hear it pop too."

The story was front-page news all over the country, and in more than one other country.

That was the beginning of Grant Silver's climb to fame: an unusually rapid climb that took him near the top of his profession's mountain with amazing speed.

He bribed and cajoled his way into the police records and full reports of the event. After a secret unapproved meeting with the first officer on the scene, Sterling managed to bribe his way into an interview with the murderer a week-and a-half after the crime.

Sterling talked to him in the prison's hospital ward where he was handcuffed to the bed rail. The man's head was still bandage-wrapped and the empty socket that had once held his left eye was covered by a grizzly looking gauze patch, kept in place by a strip of tape. There was a red blood-trail down his cheek and the bottom edge of the gauze patch was gore stained. No clever or stylish patch in his case: only what was required to prevent him from bleeding-out through his empty eye socket. Sterling learned that the killer had received numerous death threats in just the short period he'd been incarcerated: including some thinly-veiled ones from prison doctors and nurses who had been acquainted with his victims. And from others as well, including prisoners, because of the particularly heinous nature of the crime he'd committed. Surprisingly to the killer, even many hardened criminals held a soft spot for persons in the medical field: especially young female persons. In the end Sterling had managed to acquire the exclusive rights to the man's story and to produce a movie about him and what he'd done. He had to promise the killer a payment of a hundred thousand dollars for the rights. The murderer had laughed and happily bragged about what he would spend the money on when he got out. Grant Sterling had laughed along with him.

When the bandaged, half blind man asked him what was so funny, Sterling said, "You're kidding yourself. My movie will end with a doctor putting a needle in your arm while witnesses watch through a big window. I imagine some of them will be the families of the nurses you murdered. They may even cheer: that would make a really great on-screen moment. Also, I know you won't live long enough to collect the money."

Still, as soon as he arrived home Sterling called his banker and arranged for a second mortgage on his house: just in case.

The Three out of Four Murders was Grant Sterling's first hit movie. He wrote the screenplay himself. It was the first of his movies to begin with the screen emblazoned with the proclamation:

INSPIRED BY *Actual Events.*

The screen then immediately switched to what became known as: *The Sterling Oval*

After that, his movies were hits, and every one of them was promoted not as true stories, but as "Inspired by true events."

That gave him almost unlimited creative license to exaggerate or outright lie to his heart's content.

Even the title of that first hit was an outright fabrication. During the interview the killer had told him only, "I was so stoned I didn't know what I was doing." Going for something more dramatic and memorable, Sterling had falsely quoted him as saying: "I missed one, but three out of four aint't bad!" In fact, Sterling had been inspired to fabricate the dreadful fictional quote while watching **Psycho** over a huge rare steak and a twelve-pack of Coors to chase his sizable pitcher of rum and Diet Coke, all-the-while wishing he could make a Hitchcock size movie.

The lie drew every sort of response: one movie magazine critic proclaimed it was brilliant. Another very prominent critic said, "Even if it actually was said by the murderer, the quote should never have appeared in a film. It's the sort of thought that no movie-goer needs implanted in his or her brain. The critic called it the most cold, heartless line spoken on screen since Ivan Drago looked down at Apollo Creed and said, "If he dies, he dies." Though unpolished and largely false, the movie was a blockbuster hit that set the model for Sterling's future films. He became known as The King of True Stories. The general public had no idea that a great deal of what he put on the screen was unadulterated made-up bull-shit. But the money rolled in: making theater owners happy, and Grant Sterling richer and fatter.

As he was puzzling over what his follow-up to that first big hit could be, he had a long discussion with his director and old friend, Eli Hughes: who had directed all of his films: hits *and* flops. Only once in his producing career had Silver given Hughes his due credit. In an interview after the success of **The Three out of Four Killer**, Sterling truthfully said, "Eli and I are a team. When a movie is just okay it's because of both of us. When one is great, it's because of Eli."

So, when Sterling asked Hughes what he thought his next film should be Hughes shrugged and asked, "Grant, do you really intend to go with another "supposedly true" lie-fest like that one?"

"Why wouldn't I?" It was my biggest hit yet, and so far, it's had the biggest box office of any movie this year."

"Okay Grant, tell me this, "Do you mean you're willing to build a career based on untruths in films that revolve around terrible things that happen to people? Because I don't think I can."

"Eli, don't you ever look at the front-page headlines? You don't see headlines about somebody rescuing a litter of kittens from an angry Doberman. I don't have to make movies about that kind of story: Disney already does that. But if a bus full of nuns goes over a cliff: that's pure box-office gold, and money in the bank!"

"That's disgusting", Eli Hughes shook his head and said,

"Remember, I won't hesitate a second to tell you, loud and clear if I think you're going too far." "I would expect nothing less." Sterling smiled and Eli recollected the insincere smile the Cheshire Cat wore in Alice and Wonderland.

CHAPTER 3
The hits Keep on Coming

After the success of his first "true story" film, Grant Sterling developed a new morning routine. The first thing he accomplished every morning, even before breakfast, was scanning his I-Pad for potential movie material. He accomplished that while comfortably seated in the bathroom. That way he could pat himself on the back, metaphorically speaking, for taking care of two kinds of business at once. Actual back-patting had become physically impossible for him nearly a hundred pounds ago. Just one more reason why he relished the praise and adoration his films brought. The average movie-goer had no idea what he looked like: and wouldn't care anyway, as long as they liked his films. But that praise and esteem only came his way after **The Three out of Four Murders** film was a hit. That convinced him, against his own will, that he wasn't, in fact, a brilliant movie producer: he was just finally lucky enough to stumble across something that worked for him.

Despite Eli Hughes' misgivings Sterling kept digging for more awful news headlines to twist into his own personal kind of true story. Sadly, bad news was usually easy to find.

Less than two months after **The Three out of Four Murders** hit pay-dirt he came across the basis for his new "true" story.

In a little one-stop-light town in New Mexico some whacko

was burning old-folk's homes. He got away with it four times. On the fourth one a man died, which meant he was also a murderer. The authorities figured out who the arsonist was and were totally on guard and primed to take him down if he tried again. On his fifth try things didn't go at all as he planned, and his crazy spree ended.

Grant Sterling decided it would be a good enough basis for another "true" flick. Unfortunately, he found the authorities in the town not at all helpful. All he received was disgusted looks and doors slammed in his face. In this case his money didn't talk: at least not loudly enough for anyone to listen. And this time the perpetrator wasn't available to be interviewed: he had incinerated himself in a failed attempt at a fifth fire.

That didn't prevent Sterling from plowing ahead with the project. He threw together a screenplay with only the information he could scrounge up from the cable news and the internet. When he arrived at a point where he had run out of facts to use, he simply made up what he thought would look good on the big-screen. Three weeks into shooting the film, Eli Hughes walked off the set: no longer able to stomach the situation. As he left, he shouted at Grant Sterling, "We could make decent movies if you were willing to put in the work, instead of treating the audience like a bunch of idiots, rubber-necking at a car wreck! At-least our flops were real attempts to make something worth watching. What you're providing is the same kind of theater as when people used to gather in a crowd to watch a public hanging."

As he left, Sterling had shouted at his back, "Don't you think the hangmen would have sold tickets back then if they could have?"

Eli left without further comment, but the entire crew, from

cameraman to stunt coordinator nearly followed him out: skeptical that Grant Sterling could produce a hit without Eli Hughes.

Sterling did lose some of his crew, but he plunged ahead using any replacements he could find. Many in the industry were reluctant to work with him after word of Eli Hughes' defection became common knowledge.

So, two months after the start of filming, every television network in the country started showing the glitzy, extravagant trailer for the newest Grant Sterling movie:

EXTERMINATION:
INSPIRED BY TRUE EVENTS
And the now familiar:

A GRANT STERLING PRODUCTION

Cashing in on the huge success of his first "true story" movie, and gambling on a repeat hit, the major theater chains and even the 'mom & pop' drive-in theaters jumped on-board and signed on to push his new movie with all they had: and in the case of some small-town theaters, that's exactly what they invested: all they had.

And every signed contract rang Grant Sterling's cash register a little louder. He found fulfillment in the prospect of having a second box-office smash. It would prove his worth to the loud-mouth critics who blasted his work for years. And doing it without Eli Hughes would prove his brilliance all the more.

Then, lie-filled or not, **Extermination** was a hit: even a bigger hit than his first movie. Of course, a movie's success is judged not only by reviews, but even more-so by the dollar return. Which meant that all of the advance tickets purchased by movie-goers who were betting the price of a ticket that Sterling had struck gold a second time had turned it into a hit even before it opened.

As soon as the box-office reports came in Sterling called Eli Hughes to gloat. In his head he had it all planned. He'd gone through it mentally over and over till he could have recited it in his sleep. He was too busy to go see Eli in person, and wouldn't have done it anyway. He felt that a call would seem less like he was looking for Eli's approval. As it turned out even the phone call was a waste of time. All he got was a message apologizing for not being available to take calls because he was out of the country working on a film in the Bahamas. Sterling was both disappointed and angry. He was disappointed that he missed the opportunity to at least brag to Eli that he'd produced a hit without his help. He was angry both that Eli was employed so quickly, and that he hadn't been aware Eli was back at work: he felt out of the-loop.

Adding to that was learning that Eli was in the Bahamas. Grant Sterling himself hadn't been anywhere that featured sand and an ocean view for nearly a decade. His former sound technician had once told him after returning from a Hawaiian vacation that he thought he'd seen Sterling on the beach on Oahu but it turned out to be a beached whale. That was the end of beaches for Grant Sterling. It also was the end of that sound tech's employment with Grant Sterling Productions.

So, now with a pair of hits under his belt, Sterling was champing at the bit for Last Flight to be the one that would make his dream trifecta a reality.

A third hit would show to the world that he wasn't thriving solely through plain dumb luck. It would push him beyond the fluke that a single hit might be, or the coincidence of two hits. Once the rule of thrice was fulfilled, his brilliance would be proven. Then no one would give a damn if he looked like a beached whale. Just like no one cared about how much Orson Wells or Alfred Hitchcock weighed.

C H A P T E R 4
THE TRIFECTA

The first thing Grant Sterling did on the morning after the premier of Last Flight was go on-line and check the total of the domestic receipts for the movie's opening night, keeping his fingers crossed the entire time. What Sterling saw made him as happy as was Ebeneezer Scrooge upon waking in his own bed on Christmas morning.

Of course, Sterling made no attempt at a Scrooge-like happy dance. If he added the physical stress of such a foolhardy act on top of the way his heart was already pounding, he might not live to receive his Oscar at next year's awards ceremony.

He was stunned to learn that the domestic opening night receipts of **Last Flight** had actually exceeded the opening-night receipts of both **The three out of Four Murders** and **Extermination.** And there were still the foreign earnings to look forward to. He'd always felt certain **Last Flight** would be a world-beater, and he was right.

Before he was done nobody would even remember Avatar. Then he would no longer be submitted to such sarcasm and outright cruelty as being called the King of the Fat Filmmakers as he had recently been called in the cover-story of a popular industry magazine. He would no longer be humiliated by envious competitors; the ones whose careers had outshone his in the past: but would no more, of that he was certain.

Nobody can ignore dollar signs when the numbers after them get really big and are followed by a long row of zeros. He only hoped that Eli Hughes saw the box-office figures and couldn't stop thinking about them when he was on the beach in the Bahamas. Sterling even considered trying Eli's cell number, and if he got him, he would ask him how Bahamian rum goes with the crow he must be eating over walking away from a major hit. But he decided to go out for a big breakfast instead: steak, eggs, and hotcakes sounded really good, and of course a bloody Mary, since he was celebrating. He dialed up his chauffer and told him not to spare the gas getting there. He briefly gave thought to the stock Hummer in the garage: the one that was standard length and black. He hadn't driven himself since he struck gold with **The Three out of Four Murders**. Though he would never admit it to anyone else, (it nearly killed him to admit it to himself): another major reason his new-found success was a godsend was because he could finally afford a chauffeur to drive the huge, gaudy limo. The last time he had driven the normal Hummer he'd barely managed to squeeze himself into it, and for a brief moment he was terrified that he may have to dial 911 and get them to pry him out of it and rescue him. How would that have looked on the front page? He decided to wait for the limo.

CHAPTER 5
THE FOURTH ACT?

Once Grant Sterling had the rule of thrice on his side, he became even more diligent about looking for movie material. He had to find just the right story: one that was big enough news that the general public was at least aware it had happened. That made the "true story" aspect more credible.

But at the same time, he wanted a story that wasn't so heavily reported-on that the average movie-goer might peg the film as only being so much hog-wash.

By the fourth day after his huge third hit premiered, Sterling was already becoming discouraged. Several days of his morning ritual had shocked him. The last thing he'd expected was a series of days with no catastrophes to feed his falsehood-machine.

The closest thing he'd come up with was a relatively small fire in a railroad yard outside of Topeka, Kansas that had threatened to cause a massive explosion and ensuing inferno if it hadn't been extinguished before the flames reached several tank cars laden with flammable chemicals. Unfortunately for Sterling, the firefighters had done their jobs quickly and the worst hadn't happened.

Creating a close-to-true movie about the event would be relatively easy and affordable. Some computer manipulation of news videos and a few on-the-spot interviews with actors dressed as railroad employees would go a long way. And he knew of people who were experts at making believable models to set on-fire. That along with some pyrotechnics would be relatively inexpensive and would do the trick: if he was anyone else.

But turning the true story into a Grant Sterling spectacle would be a vastly different thing to pull off. Even with a happy ending the film would require blowing up or burning up some big, very expensive equipment to make it interesting enough to draw crowds. Still, out of curiosity he'd devoted some computer time to researching costs. The research told him that if he sold everything he owned and invested the total profits from his three hits, he couldn't cover the cost of making the movie he would want to make.

With a diesel locomotive costing a half-million to two-million dollars, and freight cars costing a hundred thousand to two-hundred thousand, not-to-mention the cost of renting a railroad yard and hiring real railroaders as believable extras for the film shoot. He didn't have a prayer of pulling it off. It would take a Die Hard or Indiana Jones-sized budget and a studio like 20th Century Fox or Paramount to have what it would take to make the movie: the cash and the skills. He put out a few feelers to the big studios. Fox simply wasn't interested. Paramount liked the film's basic concept, but was concerned about who would direct: They, like every other studio in town knew about Sterling losing Eli Hughes. Until then Sterling hadn't understood how highly thought-of Eli was. When Grant Sterling met with the head of Paramount, Sterling asked, "Who directed the Indiana Jones series? He knew the answer before he asked. The question was meant to see how interested in bank-rolling the project they actually might be. Paramount's president looked over his glasses at Grant Sterling for a moment, and then, smiling slightly, answered, "Stephen Spielberg, but unless you've produced a few Star Wars sized hits, you'll play Hell getting him on board. Then the man added, sarcastically, "Unless you're George Lucas you'll never get Spielberg. And without a Lucas or Spielberg, or better yet: both of them, you'll *never* get a major studio to take on this project." Then he said, "Thanks for stopping by." His face held a small sneer as he said it, and he pointed at the door. There was no offer of a handshake, or any other pleasantries: like, "have a good day." Before the door closed behind him, Grant Sterling looked at the studio head and said, "See you at the Oscars. I'll be the one heading for the stage to deliver my acceptance speech."

Before the door was totally closed, Sterling heard,

"See you there! I'll save you three seats!" He could hear the man bellowing laughter all the way to the elevator. Before he pressed the button for the lobby he checked the plastic-covered sign by the door that displayed the elevator's weight limit.

Sterling knew that there wasn't an elevator anywhere with a weight limit low enough for even his bulk to be too much.

Doing some quick math in his head as he pressed the button for the lobby, he figured that it would take over thirty people of his weight to exceed the elevator's limit.

The fact was, although he put on a show of his size not bothering him, he was truly miserable.

He wasn't miserable in the physical sense: other than his legs aching when he was on his feet more than ten or twenty minutes, he felt fine. But after years of being the punchline of a thousand jokes he'd become almost terminally self-conscious. And that led him to actions like examining elevator weight limits and even estimating the width of doorways when he was someplace unfamiliar.

Also, some soul-searching had made him realize that things would only get worse. The unexpected success of his lastthree movies had made his bank-account graduate into the nearly-bottomless category. Which meant more high-end restaurants: very few of which offered low calory choices. Even when in one of the few that did, he simply ignored that portion of the menu. His style was rich foods with a ridiculous amount of butter. That was his rule to live by: or die by. And the meal was always followed by an equally deadly desert, of course. Grant Sterling had an over-abundance of both fat and lately, cash. But he was totally devoid of will-power.

So, what if his legs hurt: he could afford all the Ben-Gay and Ibuprofen a Walgreens could fit on their shelves.

On the way home, while ignoring the small-talk his driver attempted to initiate, he thought, 'If only that railroad fire had been bigger:' If it had been, and he'd gotten it on film, it would have been the clincher with a big studio, especially with his ideas on how to make it even more spectacular. He could do as he pleased with a film that was "Inspired by Actual Events."

That night, sitting up in bed shoveling in chocolate ice cream from a bowl bigger than a dinner plate, the obvious solution hit him like a ton of bricks.

C H A P T E R 6

The Lord Helps Those Who Help Themselves

The following morning found Grant Sterling on the phone to Dylan Roberts, one of Hollywood's top pyrotechnics men. He was a wizard at blowing things up and making them burn spectacularly, but had been effectively black-balled in the city after one of his rigs went off too early and caused the death of three actors, two of them children. He wasn't found liable for the deaths, but his career was as dead as the actors who were killed in the tragedy.

When Grant Sterling called, he was surprised to get Roberts' voice mail, since he knew the man hadn't found work. He left Roberts a message saying, Dylan, please call, I have a project where I could really put your skills to good use. He left his home number and cell number. After leaving the message, Sterling went out to eat, and had his cell phone on the table within easy reach through all four courses. Breaking with his normal routine, he skipped dessert; anxious to get home and sit by the phone with a snack, in case the pyro man called.

When the call came, the first thing out of Grant Sterling's mouth was, "Dylan, old buddy, have you ever been to Kansas?"

Roberts cautiously said "Only passing through, why?"

"I just wondered," Sterling said.

"Do you have something going on in Kansas? Are you filming there?" Roberts asked somewhat hesitantly.

"I hope to," Sterling answered enthusiastically. Then he added, "If you are interested in the job I could use you."

Again, Roberts answered cautiously, "You know I haven't worked in more than a year."

"Indeed, and I think it's very unfair. All the years that you were considered the best, and one slip ruined it all." Sterling shut up, waiting for Roberts to process what he'd said.

Finally, the man answered, "Do you really thing I was treated bad?"

Sterling held his breath for a moment, trying to decide if he should correct Dylan Roberts' grammar. Then he chose not to insult the man, considering what he was going to ask of him.

Instead of an insult, he chose to lie, something he was getting very accomplished at. "Absolutely, you were. Anybody can make a mistake."

Roberts said, "Everybody's mistakes don't kill three people."

"That's a very kind, compassionate statement, considering that because of that one mistake they threw you out like last week's garbage."

Finally, Dylan Roberts asked, "Okay, why did you call? What do you really want?"

"I don't want anything, except to offer you an opportunity."

"An opportunity to what?

"To make a big chunk of cash, and possibly even get your career back on track. I pull a lot of weight in this town; with the hits I've had lately. You weren't convicted of a crime. With me reminding the studios how good you are, great things could happen."

When Roberts answered his voice was firm and his message clear, "I've never worked with you, so I only have what I've heard about you to judge by: And what I've heard is that you're at least three hundred pounds of shit in a fifty-pound sack. I had the city's best cameraman tell me he wouldn't trust you as far as he could throw you. And Schwarzenegger couldn't throw you four feet. Goodbye now."

Sterling quickly said, "Don't hang up yet! I've got fifty-thousand dollars with your name on it."

Dylan Roberts sighed heavily and said, "Where and when?"

Sterling smiled contentedly. He knew he had Roberts. A man who has lost everything that mattered to him is an easy mark. Fifty-thousand was nice bait; but Grant Sterling knew it was his vague hinting that he might be able to help Roberts get back in the game that got the pyro-man to take the bait.

Topeka, Kansas, huh?" Dylan Roberts asked Grant Sterling across the restaurant table. Roberts had only had a couple eggs and toast. He was too nervous to eat much.

The restaurant wasn't in danger of closing due to lack of business as long as Grant Sterling was there. The big man had ordered a double order of steak and eggs, with a side of pancakes. His meal had definitely balanced out Roberts' small order. After forking several huge bites into his mouth Sterling finally pushed the plates aside, and propping his elbows on the table, answered Dylan Roberts' question "Yep, I've got a project going on that is happening right outside of Topeka."

"Another of your Inspired By" pictures?"

Sterling nodded. "That's the plan. But the future of the

project could depend on your ability to handle the gig." Sterling shrugged dramatically for emphasis. Roberts nodded and said, "No problem. I can handle anything you come up with."

Sterling had baited the hook, and Roberts had taken the bait. Now it was only a matter of reeling him in. Sterling took a thick envelope from his jacket pocket and slid it across the table. He grinned a toothy grin that was barely visible between his flabby lips and said, "Fifty thousand, as promised. Roberts grabbed the envelope, and nodding, stuffed it in a hip pocket. Still wearing the cheshire-cat grin Sterling said, "I'll call you this evening with the details."

"Okay!" Roberts got up and left the restaurant. Sterling signaled for the waiter and ordered two desserts.

C H A P T E R   7
TOPEKA

At 6:20pm, as soon as he felt dusk was getting deep enough to help him stay unnoticed, a man dressed in black jeans and black long-sleeved t-shirt crept from behind a shed that was attached to an ancient brick round-house, and stepped carefully over the rusty rails that went off in all directions. He carried a duffle bag (also black). Now that he saw a light at the end of his financial tunnel; a phrase that, upon entering Dylan Roberts' head made him snicker, considering where he was). Taking out his phone, he logged onto Google Earth, and was soon looking down on the patch of land he was skulking through. As he'd been instructed to, he walked out along a specific one of the tracks that radiated from the round-house. As he'd been informed, less than thirty yards from the round-house he came to where the grass and thick weeds along both sides of the track were burned black. Even the mound of large stones that lay between the rails looked charred and grimy. Grant Sterling had certainly done some research. Again, checking his phone, he saw the overhead view was so clear he could distinguish a boxcar on a nearby siding that was burned so badly that its color was nearly indistinguishable beneath the charr. It was the one he'd been told to look for. It was the railroad car where the recent fire had started. It apparently had been pulled onto the siding to await whatever its fate would be. Dylan Roberts knew nothing about what railroad freight cars were worth, but to his untrained eye it appeared to be a total loss.

Of course, that wasn't his problem. Within a half-hour at the most he'd be finished, and the train car wouldn't matter at all; at least not to him.

Dylan Roberts looked around carefully for anyone who might notice him. He saw no one, but he did hear the wail of a train's air horn off in the distance. Knowing nothing about the typical flow of train traffic in the rail yard, he had no clue when the train he heard would arrive, if it was coming his way at all. Wanting to take no chances, he crouched down, and doing a duck-walk that would have made Chuck Barry envious, crossed multiple tracks till he was beside the fire-damaged freight car.

He dropped to his ass on the berm that rose up from the wear-worn soil along the track. He leaned down and peered up under the blackened rail car. After taking a small flashlight from the duffel bag, he examined the railcar's underpinnings.

It took only a minute for a man with his extensive, though unappreciated knowledge and skill to decide how to proceed.

Dragging the duffel bag behind him, he crawled over the nearest rail and then slid on his back between the rails till he was near the center of the car. Holding the little flashlight in his mouth to free up both hands, he removed several items from the duffel bag and went to work. He was running what Sterling had told him through his head, though Sterling had been very vague when Roberts asked questions. When he'd asked Sterling what was the point in burning an already-burned rail car, the fat man had responded with a line of double-talk that really didn't answer his question; something about it being important to the plot of the film that it look like a missed hot-spot from the original fire had ignited a second blaze. When Sterling asked him if he could do the job, Roberts said, "Sure, no problem."

Fifteen minutes after crawling under the train car Dylan Roberts was finished what he'd come there for. It was almost totally dark, with only moonlight to function in. Still, he craned his neck looking in every direction that was visible before dragging himself from beneath the railroad car. The timer would give him ten minutes to make himself scarce. He hesitated to use the flashlight. He could hear the sounds of hammers and air tools from the direction of the shed he'd previously hidden behind. For all he knew there could be a shop full of late-shift workers preparing to get off any time. He didn't relish the prospect of going to jail; or of being caught by a group of pissed-off railroad workers who were experienced in the use of large, and no-doubt dangerous, tools.

And of course, there also was the unpleasant prospect of armed security people. Just because he hadn't seen any on the way in, and had slipped in unnoticed, didn't mean he could do the same getting out. He could have easily missed spotting a watchman, or watchmen, while sneaking into the railyard. And a bullet would be far more final than a beating or jail.

When Roberts mustered up the guts to take a shot at leaving the railyard, keeping low, he eased his way across the multiple tracks, barely avoiding falling on his face several times when his foot caught on a rail. When he was finally within sight of the employee parking lot where he had parked his car as far from any building as possible, he risked moving a little faster. Only once did he turn the light on, just long enough to check his watch.

Seeing that six of the ten minutes he'd set the timer for were gone, he threw caution to the wind and sprinted for his car. He kept glancing over his shoulder as he fled, wondering if he'd overdone the load. He wanted to be in his car and a good way away before it went off. He'd known from their first meeting that Grant Sterling was pulling a snow-job on him with all his praise and pity. Though Sterling was playing him, Roberts knew he *was* one of the best. But a piece of blistering hot shrapnel whizzing through the air won't play favorites. It would kill him just as dead as it would a rank beginner. He didn't intend to take that chance. He jigged left a little as he ran, to put a row of parked cars between him and the burnt train car that would very soon be in even worse condition.

Roberts jumped in his car and slammed the door behind him. He turned the key, and the instant the engine fired up threw the shifter in drive and stomped the accelerator pedal. The car jumped forward, the wheels spinning in the gravel of the unpaved parking lot. He twisted the steering wheel, desperately trying not to lose control. Just as the car straightened up and he aimed it the exit to the highway; a huge crash, of his making, sounded from the rail yard.

Dylan Roberts saw the column of smoke rising behind him in his rear-view mirror and smiled a satisfied smile.

Less than fifty yards from where he hit the highway, he passed Grant Sterling's ridiculous silver limo sitting in a turn-out by the road.

A tall man in a uniform and cap like something from an old Perry Mason episode stood beside it with a camera bearing a long lens, pointed in the direction of the railyard. "Must be Sterling's chauffer" Roberts mumbled aloud, speaking only to himself.

As Dylan Roberts sped by, Grant Sterling flashed him an extremely pudgy thumbs-up through the back window. As he drove away from the rail-yard he wondered if Sterling could, or would, actually do anything to jump-start his ruined career. The fifty-thousand was a nice shot in the arm, but not close to balancing the risk he'd just taken on the project that Sterling kept bragging about. He still had no idea what it was, if there was really a project at all.

Grant Sterling rolled from his car, and leaning on the hood, sked his driver, "Did you get it? Is it good stuff?" The drover said, "Damned if I know. My specialty is getting the tank you're leaning on through traffic. You're the big-shot that makes "*true*" movies," he needled Sterling. "I guess you'll know when you look at what I got."

Sterling replied, "You do know chauffeurs are a-dime-a-dozen." Then he added, "You're fired!

"Well go hire a dozen; one to drive and eleven to pick you up if you fall while you're oozing out of the car." Then the man made a production of eye-balling Sterling head to toe, and said "You better hire two dozen." He then proceeded to get in the driver's seat and start the engine. He was considerate enough to not start the car moving till Sterling stopped leaning on the limo and stepped away from it.

As the huge car rolled away down the road Sterling shot it a pair of middle fingers. There was no indication that his former driver saw the gesture; No slowing, no blink of brake lights in the nearly total darkness that had by-then fallen. The only light remaining was the full moon.

If nothing else, Sterling had hoped to see a middle finger raised in response to his two-handed gesture. At least then he'd know his ex-driver saw his parting shot: not much satisfaction, but something. Sterling looked up the road in one direction, then the other, but the idea of walking left his head almost before it was there. Using his cell phone to look up the number, he dialed the limousine service that had done the conversion work on the silver Hummer. They promised to contact a service in the Topeka area and arrange to have him picked up as soon as possible. Though embarrassed, he reminded them he would need a ride that would accommodate his size. Twenty minutes later he was in the back of a white limo that was every bit as big as his own car, heading to the airport. The limo company that picked him up also arranged to have his silver Hummer driven back to Hollywood for him, since the driver who had driven him the over fourteen-hundred miles to Kansas was no longer his employee.

When he was finally on the plane home, after catching considerable grief over his size: a situation that had been resolved only when a boarding agent who was a fan recognized his name, he sipped Champaigne, and recalled one of his mother's favorite sayings; "The Lord helps those who help themselves."

He wondered if she would be proud of him now; When no suitable tragedies had occurred, he'd helped himself and made one, or at least started the process.

Back in Hollywood, after screening the not-too-terrible footage his former chauffer had shot at the Kansas railroad yard he had a talented editor punch it up and had some big-time special effects and computer-generated scenes added. Sterling was proud, and quite frankly stunned by how much his recent successes and newfound fame made people willing to work for him: big industry talents who he could never have gotten before his "Inspired By" films turned into a gold mine.

CHAPTER 8
THE BIG PITCH

Five mornings after returning from Topeka, Grant Sterling again sat in the waiting room of the office of the president of Paramount Studios doing his best to balance his alligator skin briefcase on his knees. Carrying the briefcase was totally unnecessary. It only held two things: A stack of his business cards and a computer flash-drive with the cobbled-together video that he hoped would open the door to the kind of grand production he could create with a major studio's backing. He could have carried both in a pocket, but he hoped the high-dollar brief case would make a good impression. He'd bribed the Paramount big-wig's secretary to put him on the big-wig's appointment calendar or he'd have never made it through the door. Now he was principally being ignored. Finally, he was called into the office.

The meeting was short. The big-wig did take a moment to plug the drive in this computer and watch the three-minute-long video. Then he said, "Leave me a few of your cards and I'll pass them along to some other studios who might consider doing something with it."

"But you're not interested?"

"No. I wasn't interested the last time you pitched it, and I'm not now."

"But you'll pass it on?" Sterling was whining and it pissed him off, because he knew the studio exec had no more intention of helping him than he had when he was making hollow promises to Dylan Roberts. But he kept going, practically begging.

The studio-head finally said, "Are you going to give me the cards on your way out or just go out?"

"Will you really pass them out?"

"If it'll get you to leave me alone!" He pointed at the door.

Against his every instinct, Sterling said, "Thank you so much." He almost would have gotten to his knees and bowed, but of course, he couldn't have gotten back up.

As Sterling left the office the man said, in a mock whisper intended to be heard, "See you at the Oscars."

Sterling slammed the door behind him, and rode the elevator to the parking garage where his new chauffer waited in the limo.

He knew news traveled fast in Hollywood, but was stunned to find that by the day after he lost his last driver everybody in town knew about it, and was laughing about it. Consequently, finding a driver who would work for him cost three times what he'd paid the former driver.

C H A P T E R 9
LUCKY ACCIDENT

At 2:00 pm two days after Grant Sterling was basically thrown out of the Paramount studio- head's office for the second time, he received the most surprising phone call of his life. It had to do with what was one of the luckiest accidents he'd ever heard of: and definitely the luckiest he'd ever experienced.

The caller-ID showed a number that he'd never heard of and most confusing thing of all was that the location shown was Toronto, Canada.

He assumed it was a salesperson calling to sell him insurance, or an auto warranty, or something else he had no need for. He considered ignoring it, but curiosity got the best of him and he picked it up.

The man on the other end said, "Good afternoon. Is there a chance Mister Sterling is available?"

Caught totally off-guard, Sterling said, "Available for what?"

The man nickered and said, "To take my call. I'd really like to talk to him if he's available."

Sterling blurted out, "Who do you think you're talking to?" Then wishing he could rewind time to before his mouth got totally out of control, he said, "I apologize. This is Grant

Sterling. How can I help you?"

The stranger on the phone said, "Oh, I expected to get your receptionist, or secretary."

"She's on maternity leave right now," sterling lied. I told her I'd hold her job for her, so I'm handling my own office for now. She does good work and I want to treat her right," he went on, envisioning the fictional secretary as he spoke. In his head she was a tall blond in the 36/24/36 category with long flowing locks, and full lips that required no lipstick.

The man on the phone said, "It's good to know you treat your employees so well. I like working with ethical people I can trust."

At the phrase 'working with', Sterling nearly wet his pants with anticipation. Finally, as calmly as possible he asked, "To whom am I speaking?"

"Charles London."

"Of Charles London Productions"? Sterling was so excited he hoped he didn't have a heart attack, or embarrass himself by getting so tongue-tied the words wouldn't come at all.

"Oh, you've heard of me?" the man on the phone said.

"Yes sir, I sure have!" Sterling answered, sounding like a kid on a playground. He slapped his hand over his mouth to keep from babbling on foolishly.

"I'm flattered," Charles London answered evenly. Sterling couldn't tell if he actually sounded flattered or not. He was still flabbergasted at receiving a surprise call from the owner of the largest movie production company in Canada.

After drawing a few deep breaths Sterling managed, "How can I help you, Mister London?"

As soon as he said it, he wished he hadn't sounded like a teenager asking what a drive-thru customer at McDonalds wanted to order.

I wanted to speak to you about a movie idea you pitched to my friend at Paramount."

"He told you about it?" Sterling said in disbelief. He was becoming more excited with every surprise Charles London threw at him.

Sterling herd him expel just a breath of a snicker, and his excitement instantly vaporized.

"Yeah, he mentioned it over lunch.

"What did he say about it? Did he give you my card?"

"Not exactly. Before he left the restaurant, he wrote his personal number on the back of one of his cards and gave it to me. When I flipped it over your card was stuck to it. I'm aware of your recent successful films, and thought it would be worth a call. It costs nothing to listen."

"So did he tell you anything about my project?"

"Only in very broad terms. But I would like to discuss it with you in person. Do you think you could fly up here to Toronto tomorrow or the next day?"

Grant Sterling hesitated while his head spun with images of the misery he experienced flying back from Kansas. He didn't relish the idea of spending hours hoping to find an airline employee who was a Grant Sterling fan. He'd love to be able to delude himself into believing he was world-renowned. Sadly, though he'd become a master at lying to the public; he still couldn't lie to himself that much. He couldn't ignore the obvious.

Despite his weight and size, he *was*, in fact, a small fish in a big pond. His bank account had grown with amazing rapidity. Compared to his current worth he was virtually a pauper before his "Inspired By" hits. But in Hollywood things were different than in the real world. There were big producers and directors whose worth made his seem like chump-change. Spielberg probably had more money that had fallen behind his couch cushions and not been missed. He recalled hearing a conversation between two big-wheels in the business. One of them said, "Did you hear what Oprah got for the last movie she did? What a haul!"

The other man had answered, "Everything is relative. If George Lucas woke up tomorrow and only had Oprah Winfrey's money, he'd probably jump off a building."

CHAPTER 10

A SURPRISE WINDFALL

Finally, after giving himself a long moment to conjure up a suitable lie Sterling answered, "If day-after-tomorrow is soon enough, I could probably wrap up a couple things that need my personal attention and be up there then." He paused to give himself psychological props for making himself sound important.

After a pause, Charles London said, "Okay, day-after-tomorrow. Once you've made plane reservations, call me with your arrival time and I'll have a car there to meet you."

"Mister London, I'm embarrassed to mention this, but…"

"I know: I've seen your photo in a trade-magazine. I'll take the situation into consideration when booking the car."

Glad that he was home where the gesture would be unseen by anyone, Sterling pumped his fist in the air and shouted, "Yes!"

Within ten minutes he'd contacted the limo company and asked them for the phone number of an airline they would recommend for him to charter a private plane from Hollywood to Toronto in two days. When he called to book the plane, he confided to them about his size. The booking agent said, "Don't worry, we'll handle it." His arrangements made, he fried up a three-inch-thick porterhouse, drowned it in steak sauce, and microwaved a frozen double-cheese pizza for dessert. He was performing the food equivalent of drowning his sorrows. Though the phone call from London had excited him to no end, part of the results of the call had embarrassed him to no end. Twice in less than a half-hour he'd be forced to bow down, figuratively speaking, to strangers because of his weight. First, Charles London. London had already been aware of his size, which somehow made it worse. If London had only been familiar with his work, he'd have been flattered. But he'd only recognized him as the fat guy on the magazine. He'd said he'd take the situation into consideration when sending a car.

"The Situation": like he had a disease to watch out for.

Sterling decided that during the flight north he would figure out whether to tell Charles London that big-shot movie producers can't catch fat: it's not infectious. Even as the thought crossed his mind, he discarded it. He wasn't ready to throw away an unbelievable opportunity over a presumed insult. And then he'd told the airline about it. This time around he dreaded hitting a trifecta. One more time might be more than he could handle. Before doing anything else, he phoned Charles London and notified him of when his flight would be landing in Toronto the day-after the next. Then he decided to chow-down.

As Grant Sterling had predicted, his newfound success had quickly revealed its down-side. As his bank account had grown, so had his weight and waist size. His previous three-hundred pounds had ballooned to three-twenty. He didn't know what his waist size had grown to, only that none of his pants fit anymore, and he'd had to buy a longer belt twice since the release of **The Three out of Four Murders**. Despite his previous claims to Eli Hughes about not giving a damn what people thought as long as they bought tickets, he was beginning to fear that he may have to get one of those alarm things from: the "Help I've fallen, and I can't get up!" people.

Or, worse than needing help off the floor, he was afraid he'd hit the ground hard and end up like Humpty Dumpty. Sterling knew if all the King's horses and all the King's men couldn't put him together again, he was finished. Although he really wouldn't want horses trying to put him together again: even a King's horses.

CHAPTER 11
TORONTO

The corporate jet leased by Grant Sterling descended gracefully from the clouds and touched down at Toronto's Pearson International Airport at ten-o-five am two days after the day Grant Sterling received his unbelievable call from Charles London. The price for chartering the plane was more than he would ever have believed he'd spend on a one-way flight anywhere. The combined cost of leasing the plane for the twenty-two-hundred-mile flight and paying the pilot was over twenty-five thousand dollars, more than half of what he'd paid Dylan Roberts to set an already burnt boxcar on fire as a prop for his promotional video. And that twenty-five thousand was only one-way. He also had to get back home. If he'd been a praying man, he'd have spent the entire flight praying that all the money he'd put into pitching this movie idea wasn't just flushed down the toilet. He had spent nearly the entire flight crossing and uncrossing his fingers. He did take the time to check out the paperwork on the plane lease. He discovered a line-item that showed two-thousand- dollar additional charge for unspecified customer-required costs. At least they didn't list it as a two-thousand-dollar obesity fee.

When Sterling deplaned, he immediately called Charles London to let him know he'd arrived. He got a receptionist who said London was in a meeting. She promised she would give him the message. Sterling said he would call back. Then he asked the first airport customer-service employee he ran into where he might find a coffee shop or restaurant where he could wait till his ride appeared. The beautiful young lady, who wore a blue and white blazer and a like-colored cap with the airport's logo on it, smiled and gave him a look-over. Her career had taught her the importance of watching everybody, but to do so discreetly. The girl was good; as soon as he asked the question, she bought herself a moment to think by making an intentionally noticed glance over his shoulder and forcing a rather nasty annoyed expression to cross her beautiful face, as though she saw something or someone behind him that she would have rather not seen. In the long moment it took Grant Sterling to twist around his thick neck, the girl took a long thorough look at him. When he turned back to her, she put on a well-practiced smile and said, "Let me think." She put her chin in her hand and looked around the terminal. It was obviously a trained ploy to look determined to provide excellent service while actually killing time. Finally, she nodded down the concourse and said, "There's a coffee shop a little way down on the left. But on second thought, up that way." She pointed. "Not very far is a nice restaurant, it's bigger and has nice comfortable booths." She smiled an awkward smile. Then Sterling got it! "Oh, you mean booths I can fit in without them collapsing?"

"I am sorry, sir. I meant no offence; I was only thinking of your comfort."

As he stared at her she looked oddly familiar. Then it leaped into his mind: She was a dead ringer for the fictional secretary he'd been building in his head, except with a few bonus well-placed curves.

Looking at her ID badge he said, "Well Amber, I'm here for a big business meeting. If it goes well, I could use someone to celebrate with."

He had hoped for a look of pleasant surprise, but saw only uncomfortable squinting and lip licking: clear indicators of an as-yet unspoken no. Before turning to go off toward the big comfortable restaurant she'd indicated, he said, "Amber, if the deal I've got going comes through, by tomorrow I could be a very wealthy man." Then he corrected himself, "Actually, I'm already a very wealthy man, but I expect to be a lot wealthier. I'll let you know before noon whether to dress for the classiest place you can think of. The clothes will be on me. And everything that goes with it: shoes jewelry, hair-do, the whole-ball of-wax. Then in what he thought was a smooth move, he added, "I've got a feeling you're just my type."

Saying nothing, the beautiful skycap turned on her heel and walked quickly away.

Grant Sterling walked in the direction which Amber; the beautiful but uncooperative airport chick had indicated would lead him to the nice restaurant. The one that was bigger, and had nice comfortable booths. It took him fifteen minutes to make the walk that would have taken most people five. When he arrived, he was panting like a worn-out hound-dog. When he stumbled in the hostess asked if he was okay. Judging by the concern in her voice, he must have looked terrible. She went as far as to offer to call 911. Sterling shook his head and answered, "No, I'll be fine with a few minutes rest and a cup of coffee. As he said it, he was eyeballing two things longingly; the long legs that showed below her skirt, and the mouth-watering images of the house specials featured on the menu displayed on the wall by the entrance.

Once seated in a large one-sided booth Sterling took out his phone to call Charles London

and notify him of his arrival. But as he laid the phone on the table, he glanced at the front of the menu the hostess had left. After giving it a full twenty seconds of pondering, he raised his hand, the slight movement making him gasp for breath. When she arrived, he ordered a twelve-ounce filet: rare, and cherry cheese-cake for dessert. And to make it all slide down easier he added an expensive bottle of sweet red wine. He asked for two glasses on the outside chance London would want to meet him there. Or on the even farther outside chance that Amber: the beautiful skycap walked by and he could bull-shit her into joining him. Then he again called Charles London. That time he spoke to him, and London said he would send a car for him. Before London hung up Sterling said, "Could you hold off on the ride for about a half-hour? I just ordered lunch.

The line went silent for nearly a minute, then London said, "Okay, a half-hour, but be ready when it gets there. I've got things to do."

He didn't sound nearly as pleasant as he had on his initial call. Sterling dug in, and the meal was finished with fifteen minutes to spare, so he had a second glass of wine, then a third.

Just as he sipped the last of his third glass the pretty hostess who had seated him walked up to him and said, "Mister Sterling?"

Startled, he swallowed the wine so fast he choked on it.

"Yes, I'm Grant Sterling. What is it?" he sputtered, wiping his chin with a napkin.

The hostess smiled and said, "I'm sorry I startled you. A gentleman asked me to tell a Mister Sterling that his ride to the studio is here. He said he'll be in the main-concourse parking lot. In a blue and white van, I believe."

As Sterling hoisted himself to his feet, he looked the woman up and down. Suddenly, proving he was far drunker than he'd believed he was, he grabbed the back of the chair he'd just vacated in order to stay upright. Then the wine really got the best of him and he winked at the pretty hostess and said, "What would it take to get you to come up to my hotel room later?"

Her mouth showed a hateful smirk rather than her previous sweet smile and she said, "Chloroform."

Sterling was so furious he began trembling. The restaurant hostess narrowed her eyes and said,

"Okay, now do you want me to call 911?"

Before Sterling could muster up the strength to answer, a handsome young man walked up and said, "Are you Grant Sterling?"

"Yes, who are you?"

"I'm Donnie Roth. Mister London sent me to pick you up. Are you ready to go?"

Scowling at the hostess Sterling said, "Damn right, get me the hell away from her!"

Donnie Roth smiled at the pretty hostess, shrugged and said, "There's no accounting for taste."

As Grant Sterling and the driver walked away, Sterling looked back at the girl, and said, "So you're too good to consider a big man, huh?"

She replied, "It's not your weight, it's you! You just plain creep me out. You were licking your lips more looking at me than at the menu. People that work hard for a living deserve some respect. I'd have shut you down if you were built like Arnold Schwarzenegger"

Sterling's parting shot was, "You made a big mistake bitch! I could have made you a star!"

"I'll do my best to go on!"

Donnie Roth and Grant Sterling walked away, with Roth leading the way.

Before they'd taken more than a dozen steps, Sterling said, "How far is it?" He was already panting and gasping for breath. Donnie Roth was twenty years younger than Grant Sterling, and more importantly, a hundred-and fifty pounds lighter. He looked as though he could knock out a hundred push-ups without pausing for breath.

We've got, probably fifty yards," Roth answered Then he added, "Do you think you can make it?" Sterling put his right hand on his chest and pressed the fingertips of his left hand to his neck to see how severely his pulse was racing. The look on his face told Donnie Roth all he needed to know. Roth looked around and then said, "There's a bench against the wall right over there." He gestured in the direction he meant. Before Sterling looked at the bench he asked, "Does it look like it can handle me?"

Roth said, "I'm no engineer, but it looks like it's made of steel, so I think it'll be okay."

"Are you sure," Sterling asked, nearly whining.

Shrugging, Roth said, "Come on. If you can make it to the bench, you can stay put till I go get a motorized cart. Then it's clear sailing to the parking lot."

In an unusually sincere show of gratitude Grant Sterling said, "Thank you! Thank you so much!"

Then realizing he was in the vulnerable role in the situation, he said, "You know, you're not a bad looking guy." Then he added, "I'm a pretty big man in the movie industry. He waited for a snide remark about his "big man" in the industry statement. When none came, he added, "I may be able to give you a shot if you're interested in acting."

Donnie smiled and answered, "Thank you Mister Sterling, but I'm already under contract to Mister London. He signed me two weeks after he hired me to work for him."

Sterling stared downward toward his feet: hidden from his sight beneath the belly hanging over his belt buckle. He finally mumbled, "It figures. Now where is that bench?"

Donnie stepped behind him and put an arm under each of his armpits. He said, Okay Mister Sterling, I'll be here with you the whole way. But you're going to have to walk. I'm here to help, that's all.

Sterling said, "Thank you. You sound like you've done this before."

"I worked one summer in an elder-care facility. I was officially a custodian; but I helped the nurses in emergencies if they needed help. Still, I have to say, most of those patients weighed about a third of what you do."

"But you will help me?" Sterling moaned desperately.

"Yes sir. I was told to get you to the studio; and that's what I'm going to do."

As Grant Sterling shuffled along at a snail's pace, Donnie Roth walked behind him, struggling to keep him vertical.

After nearly ten minutes of creeping along, they finally reached the bench that sat against the wall outside of the door opening into the restrooms. With a miserable groan Sterling dropped to the seat. He looked at Donnie and asked, "Does the bench look okay?"

Nodding, Donnie said, "I'll go get a cart. You don't go anywhere."

"Are you trying to be funny?"

"No, actually I wasn't: I meant it. Don't even try to get up till I get back. I'll only be a couple minutes."

Sterling released a winded sigh, and said, "You'll know where to find me." He even managed a short-lived chuckle. When Donnie returned, he was riding an electric cart with a seat on the rear that was designed to hold at least two passengers. He helped Sterling up from the bench and onto the cart's broad back seat. Then, with Donnie at the controls, the cart rolled smoothly along the wide concourse toward a distant doorway, where sunlight was shining welcomingly outside.

Grant Sterling said, "We're almost there, aren't we." It wasn't said in his previous whining tone. He almost seemed excited.

"Yes sir," Donnie answered. How did you know? Where you're sitting you have a good view of where we've been but not of where we're going."

"When I heard the door slide open in that direction, I felt the breeze blow past."

"Yep, you're right. We'll be in the van in no time."

Sterling said, "Good, based on that little breath of air, I think I like the way Canada smells."

Donnie maneuvered the electric cart between rows of parked vehicles, eventually coming to a stop beside an ambulance that had been repainted blue and white

"CHARLES LONDON PRODUCTIONS" was Emblazoned on the side. While Sterling leaned on the side of the vehicle peering at him, Donnie went to the back, and with Grant Sterling peeking around the corner of the big vehicle he swung open the door. Then he reached in and pushed a switch that was hidden from Sterling's view behind the frame the door hung on.

A steel ramp slid out from below the bumper.

Sterling growled, "What in the hell is that?"

A wheelchair ramp." Donnie answered.

Sterling said, "In case you haven't noticed, I'm not in a wheelchair!" Then he added, "I'm obese, but I *can* walk."

"It's a good thing, cause you're going to walk up this ramp," Donnie said, definitively. I told you before I'm here to help, but I've got a movie contract: I'm not going to end up in traction! Now get up and walk. Mister London is a busy man. If you don't get moving, you'll miss your meeting, and I'll be in trouble for letting you be late."

Where will I sit?"

"There are bench-seats on both sides, where the medical techs sat. They are big and they'll hold you. This thing is usually used to haul gear to movie shoots. You don't think we have this sitting around for taxi use, do you?"

Sterling asked "What time is it? Am I going to be on time for my meeting?"

You've got almost an hour, and the studio is only ten minutes away. Now come on!

"Right!" Sterling grunted, as he hauled himself to his feet."

CHAPTER 12
MEETING

A half-hour later Grant Sterling sat across a table from Charles London.

Before they started discussing business London had his secretary plug the flash drive Sterling brought with him into the high-tech viewing system. Within seconds one entire wall lit up and began showing a tremendously enlarged playback of what was on the flash drive.

Though grainy due to the enlargement and because it was the rough video shot by Sterling's former driver, it was clear enough to follow what it showed as they watched. Sterling mentally kicked himself for not finding a way to add an audio track to the video. With the proper audio equipment, it could no doubt have been accomplished. But he had been so focused on getting the right video that the audio aspect had totally slipped his mind.

When the brief video ended, Charles London leaned back in his chair and said, "Not bad, not bad at all.

"So, you like it!

London nodded and said, "Frankly, I like it a lot more than I expected to. Your recent work comes across as exploitation. I'm not a big fan of the kind of movies you've been making."

Sterling felt tears welling up behind his eyelids. "So, you *aren't* interested?"

Charles London said, "Let's not get ahead of ourselves.

I said I wasn't a fan of your movies, and that's a fact. But I am a fan of making money, and that's also a fact.

There's no doubt you have found your niche in the business of making profitable movies." London added.

"So, you *are* interested?" Grant Sterling said, the excitement clear in his voice. Nearly gasping for breath, he slapped his hand to his chest.

"Calm down, Charles London said, coolly. "We might work together; but not if you have a stroke before the contract is signed."

Rather than calming him, the statement stunned him as white as a sheet, and he said, "Contract!"

London nodded, a small smile on his face. He said, "If you will guarantee that you can produce a real money-maker, I'm interested. What kind of budget do you foresee it taking to produce a winner?

When Sterling seemed at a loss for an answer, London went on: Do you think two million US dollars would suffice?" Then he added, "That would, of course, also be with the aid and resources of my production department."

Sterling nodded so violently his neck cracked audibly.

Then London said, "Just one thing, who will be directing? I understand Eli Hughes isn't with you anymore"

Caught totally off-guard, Sterling said the only thing he could think of, "I'll be directing."

London suddenly didn't seem so optimistic. "You'll be producing and directing? Have you ever directed a movie before?"

Pulling out his new, but rapidly-growing skill at lying, Sterling said, "I was producer *and* director of two of my last three movies. I just gave Eli director's credit because of our long friendship"

"Oh, that's very impressive." London reached across the table and extended his hand.

With his own hand trembling so badly that he feared missing London's hand, Grant Sterling carefully reached out and shook it, all-the-while nearly swooning at the thought that his ship had finally come in, and a huge ship at that! For just a moment he thought '*Titanic sized*. Then recalling the Titanic's fate, he pushed that image away fast.

CHAPTER 13
AFTER THE DEAL

With the deal made and sealed with a handshake, Charles London pressed a button on his phone and told his secretary, "Please have Donie Roth bring the special unit around to the front entrance, so he can take Mister Sterling to his hotel."

Then he looked at Sterling and said, "I'll have the contract drawn up and delivered to your hotel in the morning, and she'll get the information necessary to transfer the money to your account. Then all that will remain will be Donnie driving you to the airport so you can make your flight arrangements. Does that sound okay with you?"

"Yes sir, absolutely!" Sterling said and then bit down hard on his tongue to keep from babbling on like an idiot.

He knew that if he blew this shot; the next thing he'd do is get a gun and blow his own brains out. He breathed deeply to calm himself down and wasn't certain he'd be able to manage it.

Just then Charles London's secretary buzzed him to report that Donnie was there to pick him up. It was exactly what he needed to briefly distract him from the situation. He would never have imagined that his unexpected new-found success could be such a challenge to deal with. He was suddenly stricken with what he'd heard called, "success stress."

He hoped his heart would keep beating long enough for him to enjoy his suddenly-brighter future.

Sterling was surprised to find Donnie Roth waiting in the hall outside Charles London's office. Donnie smiled an affable smile and said, "You ready to hit the road, Mister Sterling?"

Returning the young man's smile, Sterling replied, "You bet your ass I'm ready! I'm more ready than I've been in more than ten years, and a hundred pounds or more!"

"Okay, let's hit the road!" Donnie stepped up beside him and took ahold of his elbow. Sterling looked at the young man, and with tears trying to make themselves visible said, "Thank you Donnie. You're a good boy."

Thanks, but I'm twenty-eight years old. I hardly qualify as a boy anymore."

"No matter, Sterling answered. You're a good guy, and I think I have a job for you."

"Mister Sterling, I told you I'm already under contract to Mister London."

"I'm not talking about acting. Something totally different; and I'll pay well."

"How well?" Donny asked warily.

Let me ask you, Sterling said, "How much do you know about vehicles?"

"I know I'd rather have a Ferrari than a Yugo."

"I don't mean what you'd like to have. I mean mechanically."

"I can handle a wrench. When I was young, I learned enough to keep my cars running. And that was a lot. My first few cars were second-hand junk, or sometimes third-hand. It was either learn to fix them or walk."

Donnie paused and then asked, "What does that have to do with anything?"

"I've been thinking about a movie project," Sterling whispered conspiratorially. I'll still have to do some research and planning. I'll get at it as soon as I'm home. And you're flying to Hollywood with me.

"I don't know," Donnie said, hesitantly. "I can't do that without clearing it with Mister London."

"I'm sure he won't mind. He'll hear about it soon enough."

Donnie looked unconvinced.

Grant Sterling said, "If you help me with this project, you'll be able to buy the car of your dreams, I guarantee it."

"You can afford to say that?"

"Hell yes, I'm a millionaire!"

CHAPTER 14
BACK IN HOLLYWOOD

Warned of Grant Sterling's return to Hollywood his new driver had the long silver Hummer limo ready and waiting when the chartered plane rolled up to the gate at the airport terminal. Donnie, who had, against his better judgement, agreed to accompany Sterling, went into the terminal and returned with a motorized cart capable of handling Sterling's bulk.

After a half-hour of planning how to proceed, Grant Sterling and Donnie Roth were finally seated in the limo.

The driver asked Sterling, "Where to?"

"Home, I'm about starved." he replied.

Later, when Sterling and Donnie were seated at the big dining room table, Donnie asked, "Okay, why am I in Hollywood instead of Toronto?"

"To help me become the most famous movie producer in the world."

"And, how will I do that?"

"All you will have to do is help me set up a scene for what will be the most famous action sequence ever."

"You're really building a list of most famousness, aren't you?"

"Yes, and I'm confident the list will grow. And you'll benefit too, Donnie.

"Great, I'm up for anything to help make a movie, short of breaking the law.

Sterling fell silent, then laughed and said, "I wouldn't think of it."

"Good," Donnie answered. Sterling said, "Let's go into the living room and have a drink while I tell you about my plans."

Donnie nodded and then helped Sterling rise from his chair and they went to the living room.

Sterling downed two gin-and-tonics while Donnie nursed one beer. Then Grant Sterling dropped his bomb.

Donnie yelled, "You're out of your goddamn mind!"

Sterling nodded calmly and said, "I thought you said you'd do anything to help make a movie."

"No, I said I'd do anything short of breaking the law!"

Sterling rolled his eyes, and nearly whining, said "Donnie I thought we had the beginnings of a real friendship."

Donnie shook his head. "I didn't know you were a psycho then! I thought you were going to make a movie about a fire in a railyard."

Sterling muttered, "I was; I mean, I will. And you'll be involved. I want to do this other film first; I think it holds the most promise."

"Sure, the promise of a place in hell!"

Donnie stood and started toward the door.

Sterling, in a futile attempt at bullying him, practically shouted, "I don't know where you think you're going. You came here in my limo. And you don't think I'm going to let my driver take you back, do you?"

Donnie took two steps toward Sterling, who nearly fell over backwards backing away from him.

Donnie didn't touch Sterling, only bent low enough to be face to face with him and said in no-uncertain terms, "I'll Walk!"

"It's five miles to town."

"Good! It'll give me time to decide what I'm going to do."

"What do you mean," Sterling asked frantically.

"You can't possibly ask me what you asked me and expect me to forget about it!"

"I'll pay you a lot if you come down with amnesia.

Bill Gates doesn't have enough money to get me to forget that."

Grant Sterling growled, "I don't give a damn. I've got enough money to get *someone* to do what I want; I've already got someone in mind. And once it's done, I'll pay someone to give me an alibi.

Then I'll make the most famous action movie ever."

CHAPTER 15
INSANITY FOR FAME

On the same night, in two towns nearly fourteen hundred miles apart, two worthless money-hungry thugs went about Grant Sterling's business.

Outside of Topeka, Kansas Dylan Roberts: the **pyro-guy** again crept across the mostly deserted railyard. His target was again the burnt-out boxcar, but it had been moved to a different siding. He had no trouble locating it. The moon was full which made spotting the car easy, but required him to move more slowly and carefully, in an attempt to avoid being noticed. Every sound, even that of a frog in the distance or the rustling of a wind-blown leaf made him freeze till it passed. He made it to the boxcar and again slid beneath it dragging his bag along. Ten minutes later he crawled out. He still had his bag, but it was lighter than when he'd crawled under the train car.

Within ten minutes of Dylan Roberts doing his chore: another man crawled under an old school bus, repainted gray, and with:; Holy Trinity Monastery stenciled on the side in gold letters.

He was under the bus even less time than Roberts was beneath the rail car.

Grant Sterling sat at home watching the clock and feeding his face. When the alarm clock sounded Sterling knew the deeds had been done.

The results of Dylan Roberts' activities would be seen very soon.

What John Jenkins, the mechanic who took care of Sterling's limo had done wouldn't be known till the next morning.

Ten minutes after Dylan Roberts crawled from under the rail-car he sat on a hill that looked down at the silent, still train-yard. He had a high-tech video camera at the ready This time Sterling wanted more from him and paid him a lot more to get it.

Roberts kept an eye on his watch, much as Sterling had been watching the clock at home in Hollywood. When the alarm on his watch chirped, he grabbed the camera and got to his feet. A minute later the old burnt-up boxcar didn't just burst into flames, it exploded into a thousand pieces, flinging burning wood and metal in all directions.

A flaming chunk of wood nearly the size of a car door landed on the track next to where the burning rail-car sat. Within seconds, the old creosote-soaked wooden ties caught fire. The fire grew fast, fed by the creosote on the ties and years of grease and oil soaked into the soil and weeds around and between the rails. Within minutes the heat had grown so intense the steel rails began to warp and twist. As Roberts watched, a short, but fast-moving passenger train rounded a bend and headed for the damaged, flaming section of track. Dylan Roberts kept filming. Before the moving train hit the damaged portion of the rails, the engineer spotted the damage and locked down the brakes. Trains don't stop on-a-dime. It had slowed down a lot before it hit the bad track. When it did, reach the damaged section the locomotive and the two cars behind it derailed. The locomotive ended up on its right side on one side of the track. The derailed passenger cars landed on their left sides on the other side of the track.

Dylan Roberts took off. He jumped in his car and hit the gas. Just as he left the parking lot and hit the hard-pack, his phone rang. He grabbed it and yelled, "What?"

On the other end Grant sterling shouted, "Did it happen?"

Roberts said, "It happened and a half. I think we must have killed people!"

Sterling simply asked, "Did you get it on film?"

"Yeah, I got it!

"Okay, you rent a car and head here. And take damn good care of that camera! That's a big part of my next film: "**<u>HELL ON RAILS</u>** "Inspired by actual events". Sterling wore a smile to bed.

The following morning a little after six am an old gray school bus that belonged to a monastery near San Diego slid off a high curve and plunged down a cliff when the brakes failed. The only person on board was the priest who served as driver for staff outings. He was killed. Fortunately, the day's trip to a convention was postponed at the last minute or there would have also been eighteen nuns on the bus. That fact wasn't immediately known.

Grant Sterling saw the news of the bus crash after breakfast and said to no one but himself, "Two for two. All I'll need is a title."

Around noon Sterling's phone rang. The caller ID

Told him it was Eli Hughes. Sterling picked up and said, "Hello Eli, calling to ask for your job back?"

"No, I just wondered if you saw the news about the monastery bus going over a cliff."

Sterling said, "Yeah, damn shame: all those nuns dying." He sounded nothing like sad about it.

"Well, some updates just came on the TV news. There wasn't a single nun on the bus. Their event was canceled. The driver died."

"That's a big damned shame."

Eli asked, "What, that the driver died, or that a bunch of nuns didn't?" Then he paused for a moment before continuing, "You know, I think I recall you saying the last time I saw you that a bus-full of nuns going over a cliff would be box-office gold."

Sterling said, "I don't recall saying that." Then he asked, why don't you come over now and we'll have a few drinks and talk over old times?"

Eli Hughes said "Not right now Grant. I've got to contact the police. It's really important."

Grant Sterling grabbed his chest and toppled from his chair.

Within an hour of Eli Hughes calling the authorities, Grant Sterling did what he'd been so afraid of doing for so long. Deciding not to stay around, he wobbled into the garage and fought his way into the driver's seat of the black Hummer, with plans of hitting the road. Once he'd squeezed himself into the Hummer, he pushed the button on the door-opener clipped to the sun vizor. But over the rumble of the door going up twelve feet away, he heard the distant shriek of sirens growing rapidly closer. He pushed the button again and the light on the remote didn't come on, and the door didn't move. The screaming the siren could be no more than a block away. Panicked, Sterling turned the ignition key. The instant the engine fired up he slammed the big vehicle into gear and hit the gas. Its tires smoking on the concrete floor, Sterling's Hummer hit the garage door. The door burst outward in a hail of sheet metal and plastic.

By the time the Hummer was past where the door had been, sterling saw dozens of his neighbors crowded onto his lawn. More than a few of them had their phones out and pointed at him, recording the spectacle. Leaning on the horn to scare the rubberneckers out of the way, he headed down the driveway, gaining speed as he went. When he reached the end of the driveway, Sterling saw that the wreckage of his garage door had been thrown clear into the middle of the main road. Turning right, heading away from the city, he punched the gas again and sped in the direction of Griffith Park. As he drove away, he looked in the mirror and saw that the crowd on his lawn had grown; a lot. Many still had their phones aimed at his garage. But just as many were pointed at the Hummer. As his tires crunched over the debris of the destroyed garage door he mumbled, "That would have looked great on film".

He slammed the pedal to the floor and the Hummer charged ahead. He had a momentary thought that the Hummer didn't accelerate as fast as it used to. Then, remembering that he hadn't driven it for nearly a year, the depressing idea that hit him was, "Have I gained so much weight the car can't handle it?" As he sped on, the wail of sirens coming from behind him was rapidly growing louder.

The gates to Griffith Park were closed, as he had feared they might be. He felt no reluctance whatsoever as he threw the Hummer in reverse and backed up twenty yards or so. It probably wasn't necessary considering what he was driving, but he was in too deep to risk failing.

What he did next also wasn't necessary, but he did it anyway. He jammed the selection lever into four-wheel drive and again floored the gas pedal. Because the surface beneath the Hummer was loose, it took a moment for the four huge tires to get a grip on it, then the big vehicle lunged forward. The Hummer slammed into the gate with a resounding crash. The chain tasked with keeping troublemakers out wasn't up to the job. The chain landed twenty feet away, with the shattered padlock still hooked through its links

Grant Sterling had no real plan, but found himself drawn to the giant Hollywood sign he could see on the hill. He was running on auto-pilot, He was helpless to think of anything but the huge letters looking down on Tinseltown, from above. He didn't know what he would do if he reached the sign. His thoughts had become the mental equivalent of tunnel-vision. The huge sign was a flame: and he had become a suicidal moth.

Over the years that he had lived in Hollywood he'd visited Griffith Park dozens of times. He knew that somewhere farther into the park a service road branched off from the main road and circled the hill, climbing up behind the Hollywood sign, to allow for a service crew to reach the giant letters if necessary.

With the wailing sirens rapidly growing closer behind him, Sterling tried to stay focused on what was ahead and how to reach his goal, while at the same time, firing looks in the mirrors, to see how near his pursuers were. At one point, when he saw the rooster-tail of dust rising from the passing of his big Hummer, then immediately looked again at the huge sign before him he thought. "I'm a three-hundred-pound missile aimed at a target that I won't know what to do with if I do reach it. As romantic as the situation sounded in his head: like something a really great screen-writer could turn into a hit; he knew that what was closer to the truth was the old line about a dog that chased cars, and wouldn't know what to do with one if it caught it.

Even as the sirens and flashing lights seemed on the verge of slamming into his back bumper, he spotted the turn-off onto the service road. He knew it led off in the direction of the sign; beyond that he'd be playing it by ear. The service road was blocked by a gate. That didn't concern him. This gate looked small and flimsy compared to the one he'd already run through like a runaway train. That image was another he'd have loved to put on the big screen. But he knew he'd thrown away all chances of ever making a runaway train movie; or any other movie for that matter.

The road up the hill made a big loop on its way toward the enormous, world-famous sign.

Sterling gunned the engine and the Hummer charged up the service road throwing up road debris behind all four tires.

Though he'd seen it, and dreamed of the Hollywood sign for years; he'd never seen it from behind. When he was at the top of the service road he slowed and eventually came to a stop.

Now that he was there, he realized that he had no clue why he'd made such a mad dash, and such a maniacal effort to get there.

He looked at the back of the sign and discovered that thick steel cables ran from the tops of the letters to anchors set in large concrete pads poured in the ground twenty or thirty feet away from the sign. He'd always thought of the sign as a giant, gorgeous beacon and a tribute to what made the city, and his profession, superior to any other.

Now, sitting in the Hummer and feeling the thrum of the idling engine through his body, everything seemed impossibly different. First his incredible rise to incredible fame that would very soon evaporate like smoke. Nothing was as it had been when he crawled out of bed, feeling on top of the world. Then Eli put two and two together after hearing of the bus crash.

Now it was as though the sign existed only to taunt him.

Without making a conscious decision to do so, Sterling stomped on the accelerator and drove toward the back of the sign. He was heading toward the back of the last letter in the sign: the giant **D,** and as he drew closer, he noticed something he hadn't previously spotted. Two of the letters, the H and the W, had two cables holding them at the top. He guessed because they were bigger and wider they needed extra support. Since the D, which had only one cable was closer, that became his target. Not the letter itself, but the anchoring cable. He punched it, and headed for the cable, wondering if the cable would be any more of a challenge for the Hummer than the two gates had been. When he was only seconds from striking the cable, he heard a screaming siren from behind him. Looking in the rear-view mirror, he was shocked to see a California state Police SUV stopped fifty feet behind him, the blue lights on the light-bar on its roof throwing blindingly bright flashes that were painful to look at even in the mid-afternoon daylight. Peering more closely in the mirror he saw there was a man in camouflage fatigues leaning from the shotgun seat window. But what he had leveled on Sterling wasn't a shotgun. It was a rifle with a muzzle that looked to Sterling like the business end of a canon.

Then, even over the still-shrieking siren, a greatly amplified voice that Grant Sterling wouldn't have expected in a thousand years rang out: "Come on Grant. This isn't a movie! It's real life! And if you don't knock off the shit, they'll put a very real bullet in you!" As Sterling stared in the mirror, a man stepped from behind the SUV.

Cautiously watching Sterling, Eli Hughes lifted a bull-horn to his lips and repeated, "Knock it off Grant! It's over! Come on out and get it over with!" After a long moment with no movement from Sterling, Eli added, "Is this the way you want to be remembered by Hollywood: the hit-maker turned psycho?"

The driver's side window slid down and the Hummer's key flew out and made a small puff of dust when it hit the ground. Then, expending a great deal of energy to do so, Sterling twisted in the seat enough to stick both arms out the window and turned his hands over to show they were empty.

Then, at a loss for other ideas, Sterling opened the door and with a herculean effort swung his legs out of the vehicle.

Eli's voice cut through the air, "Smart move Grant! Now come on out and face the music! Be a man. Do what a movie hero like Arnold Schwarzenegger would!"

Sterling screamed, "I'm sick of being compared to that muscle-bound fool. He couldn't put two words together on camera if he didn't have a director telling him what to say!

Though Eli's intention had been to get Grant sterling to man-up and face the music.: he got the same outcome as a result of Sterling's anger.

With one last furious push Grant Sterling shoved himself from the hummer. As he did, he again screamed. This time his target was Eli, "Goddamn you Eli! It killed you to see me successful without you, didn't it?" When Sterling's feet hit the ground, his left knee made an impossible bend in a direction it wasn't meant to go. The eight inches of extemporaneous fat around the joint wasn't enough to prevent his knee from folding up, nor to muffle the sound of the bones in his leg shattering. The police heard the sound clearly, as did Eli Hughes.

Eli shouted at the cops, "Call for help!" As soon as he yelled it, he ran toward Grant sterling, lying face-down in the dirt. When he reached Sterling, he bent over the huge man on the ground and said, "Stay put Grant. I'll stay with you till help arrives."

Grant Sterling looked up at Eli and said, "Thank you Eli. I suppose I shouldn't have fired the sound tech who called me a beached whale. That's what I am, except this doesn't look like a beach."

"What were you planning to do to the sign, Grant?"

"Damned if I know. I guess I didn't want people to see the sign and think about me and all the stupid things I've done. I was just jealous of all the people who built successful careers, and did it the right way. I just wanted the sign gone."

Grant, there a re homes in the valley below. If those big letters slid down on them, it could have killed someone!

Sterling said" Would've made a great movie, wouldn't it!?"

EPILOGUE

Grant Sterling was found guilty of three counts of first-degree murder in the deaths of the bus driver, as well as the engineer and one passenger on the derailed train.

He was also found guilty of eighteen counts of attempted murder for conspiring to cause the death of the nuns who were supposed to be on the bus. He was sentenced to twenty years to life in a federal penitentiary. He lost fifty seventy pounds in the first month of incarceration due to food he said was worse than hospital food.

Both Dylan Roberts and John Jenkins were found guilty of various multiple felonies, iIncluding felony murder and were imprisoned for lengthy prison terms

Donnie Roth starred in a Charles London action film and became a huge star.

The biggest summer blockbuster that year was:

<u>THE TRAGEDY MAKER</u>
A TRUE *STORY*

AN ELI HUGHES PRODUCTION

THE END

About this book:

The idea for this book came to me after watching the movie "We Are Marshal."

It's about the crash of the plane that carried the Marshal University football team and coaches and many family members and boosters on November, 14,1970. At the beginning of the film it says, "this is a *true* story"

Not **based on** or **inspired by**, but: *a* true *story*. And I know it's true because Marshal University is in Huntington, West Virginia. I live in Martinsburg, West Virginia. We're clear across the state. I was in my senior year in high school when the crash happened. It touched everybody in the state. When the principal announced that all seventy-five people on the plane died, people were walking through the school crying pathetically: students, as well as teachers and staff. As quickly as possible the university staff and instructors studied the passenger manifests trying to determine exactly who was aboard the plane. It was soon confirmed that all people on the plane had lost their lives.

I know it is a *true* story.

Thanks for reading. I hope you enjoyed the book. And I hope you will say a prayer for those who were lost in the Marshal plane cash, as well as their families and friends. Some hurt doesn't go away over time.

Eddie

www.ingramcontent.com/pod-product-compliance
Lightning Source LLC
Chambersburg PA
CBHW031416310726
48971CB00003B/887